BLOSSOMING OUT

by E. S. Mooney
Story by Amy Keating Rogers
and E.S. Mooney
Based on
"THE POWERPUFF GIRLS,"
as created by Craig McCracken

SCHOLASTIC INC.

New York   Toronto   London   Auckland   Sydney
Mexico City   New Delhi   Hong Kong

ISBN 0-439-16022-7

Special thanks to Don Bishop for cover and interior illustrations

Cover design by Mary Hall
Interior design by Peter Koblish

12 11 10 9 8 7 6 5 4 3 2 1   0 1 2 3 4 5/0

Printed in the U.S.A.
First Scholastic printing, October 2000

SUGAR . . .

SPICE . . .

AND EVERYTHING NICE . . .

These were the ingredients chosen to

create the perfect little girl.

But Professor Utonium accidentally

added an extra ingredient to

the concoction —

CHEMICAL X!

And thus, The Powerpuff Girls were born!

Using their ultra superpowers,

BLOSSOM,

BUBBLES,

and BUTTERCUP

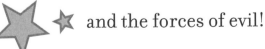

have dedicated their lives to fighting crime

and the forces of evil!

chapter 1

The City of Townsville. It's another happy day at Pokey Oaks Kindergarten. The Power-puff Girls — Blossom, Bubbles, and Butter-cup — are practicing their ABCs. Even superheroes need to learn their letters!

"All right, children, let's all try to make the letter S," Ms. Keane, the teacher, instructed the class.

Blossom picked up her red crayon. She carefully made a perfect S on her paper. "There," she said, smiling proudly.

Bubbles held her blue crayon. "I like S," she said. "S is for singing and sweetness and sugar!"

Buttercup grabbed a green crayon. "Yeah, and for socking and smashing and slamming!" she added with a grin.

And don't forget, S is for superheroes like you, Girls!

Elmer Sglue, another kid in the class, was sitting beside Buttercup. "I can't do it," Elmer sighed. "Every time I try, it comes out wrong! I give up."

"Don't feel bad, Elmer," Blossom said from across the table. "Everybody has trouble sometimes. Just keep trying, and you'll get the hang of it, I'm sure."

"Why, Blossom, what a helpful thing to say," Ms. Keane commented. "That's a very grown-up attitude."

Blossom smiled. She loved Ms. Keane. "Here, Elmer," she said, moving to a seat near him. "I'll help you practice."

Ms. Keane patted Blossom's head. "Blossom, I can count on you to help out in the classroom." She smiled. "Why, I could practically make you my assistant teacher!"

Blossom's chest puffed up under her pink dress. She felt so proud.

That afternoon, Blossom, Bubbles, and Buttercup flew home from school. As the three little superheroes flew in the door, Professor Utonium stepped out of his laboratory to greet them. The Professor had originally created the Girls in his laboratory from a mixture of sugar, spice, and everything nice — and a little bit of Chemical X. Now he was like their father.

"Welcome home, Girls. How was school today?" the Professor asked.

"Okay, I guess," Buttercup replied with a shrug. "I got in a fight with Mitch Mitchelson at recess and pushed him in the mud."

The Professor frowned. "Now, Buttercup, I've talked to you about not getting into fights."

"I told her she should just try to talk it out with Mitch," Blossom said.

"A very good suggestion, Blossom," the Professor replied. He turned to Bubbles. "How about you, Bubbles? What did you learn today?"

"Well, Ms. Keane tried to teach us the months of the year," Bubbles replied. She looked down at her shoes. "But I didn't hear everything she said. I was busy making a pretty picture of two bunnies."

"I told her that next time she should save her picture to finish later so she can pay better attention to the teacher," Blossom said.

"Another very good idea, Blossom,"

the Professor said. "You always take such good care of your sisters. You're so grown-up and responsible." He smiled. "Now, who wants an after-school snack?"

But just then there was a loud beeping sound.

Oh, no, it's the hotline! And just when the Girls were about to enjoy a snack!

Blossom flew over to the hotline. It was a special telephone that the Mayor of Townsville used to get in touch with the Girls. Blossom picked up the receiver. "Hello?"

"Powerpuff Girls, help!" the Mayor cried from the other end of the line. "A monster is attacking the Townsville Sports Stadium!"

"We'll be right there!" Blossom promised. She hung up and turned to her sisters. "Come on, Girls! Townsville needs us!" She flew off through the door.

"I'm right behind you!" Buttercup shouted, zooming after her.

"Sorry we can't stay for the snack, Professor!" Bubbles called out as she flew off after her sisters.

"Don't worry, Girls, I'll keep it waiting!" the Professor hollered after them. "Good luck!"

The Girls soared toward Townsville Sports Stadium, with Blossom in the lead.

Look at those familiar streaks of pink, blue, and green in the sky! Townsville's talented and terrific trio, The Powerpuff Girls, are on the job again.

The monster was covered with tangled-looking yellow fur and had three heads. He stood in the middle of the Townsville Sports Stadium, holding a baseball player in each of his hands. The monster roared, and sticky yellow goop dripped out of his mouth. People in the bleachers screamed and ran.

"Come on, Girls!" Blossom called to her sisters. "Let's get him!"

Blossom barreled into the soft, flabby stomach of the monster, knocking the wind out of him.

"Take that!" she cried.

The monster buckled, spewing ooze from his mouths. He dropped both players as he clutched his stomach.

"Okay, field those grounders, Girls!" Blossom instructed her sisters.

Bubbles and Buttercup zoomed down, each catching a player in midair. Then Blos-

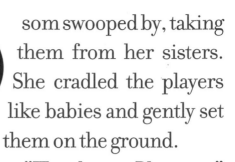

som swooped by, taking them from her sisters. She cradled the players like babies and gently set them on the ground.

"Thank you, Blossom," the players said gratefully before heading into the dugout.

The monster staggered to his feet. He bellowed a bone-chilling cry.

"You don't scare me!" Blossom cried, zooming back at him. "Come on, Girls!" she called. "Time for batting practice!" She grabbed baseball bats and tossed them to her sisters.

Bubbles and Buttercup pounded the monster's heads with the bats.

"Okay, make way," Blossom instructed. "I'm coming in to pinch-hit!"

"No way!" Buttercup replied. "I'm not finished yet!"

"Buttercup, get out of the way," Blossom instructed. "I'm going to hit this one out of the park."

"Do you really have to?" Bubbles said sweetly. She looked at the monster, who was sitting on the pitcher's mound with his middle head in his furry yellow hands. "He looks really sorry now."

"Bubbles, whose side are you on, anyway?" Blossom sighed. Sometimes her sister could be so stubborn. "Watch out, I'm going for a grand slam!"

Blossom zipped toward the monster, holding the bat tightly.

POW! "Strike one!" she cried. *CRACK!* "Strike two!" She smacked the monster again. "Strike three and you're outta here!"

Blossom yelled. She swung as hard as she could. The monster flew into the air and sailed out of the ballpark. Soon he was just a tiny dot in the sky.

"Well, that takes care of him!" Blossom dropped her bat and straightened out her pink dress.

The crowd cheered. The Mayor of Townsville was standing among them. He was dressed in his usual top hat and official Mayor's sash.

"Great job! Townsville thanks you!" he said happily. He patted Blossom on the back.

"Blossom, you're a true hero! I don't know what we'd do without you."

Once again, Blossom's chest swelled with pride.

Great job, Blossom! What a super superhero you are!

chapter 2

Later that night . . . the three Powerpuff Girls lay in bed together, sleeping peacefully and dreaming of — Hey, wait a minute! What are you doing awake so late, Blossom?

Blossom tossed and turned. On one side of her, Bubbles slept with her arms wrapped around her stuffed octopus, Octi. On the other side of the bed, Buttercup swung her fists and scowled in her sleep.

Blossom thought about her day. She heard the Mayor's voice echoing in her head. *"Blossom, you're a true hero! I don't know what we'd do without you."*

Then Blossom remembered what the Professor had said to her that afternoon. *"You always take such good care of your sisters. You're so grown-up and responsible."*

Finally, Blossom remembered Ms. Keane's kind words. *"Why, I could practically make you my assistant teacher!"*

Blossom beamed with happiness. The grown-ups were all so proud of her. They all counted on her. Why, she was practically a grown-up herself!

Blossom looked at her sisters again. She thought about Bubbles and her silly babbling. She thought about Buttercup and her tomboyish fights. Her sisters were almost like babies compared to her!

Blossom fell asleep with a smile on her face . . . a very grown-up smile.

The next morning!

As the first rays of sun streamed through the window, Bubbles sat up in bed and rubbed her blue eyes.

"What a pretty day filled with pretty sunlight," she sighed happily. "I just know we're going to have tons of fun today!"

Buttercup jumped up and grabbed her green bed pillow. "Pillow fight!" she yelled, smacking her sisters with it.

Bubbles giggled as the pillow bounced off her blond pigtails.

Blossom sat up in bed. "Do you two mind?" she said in

her most grown-up voice. "I am trying to get some sleep!"

Bubbles giggled again. "But Blossom, it's morning."

"Yeah," Buttercup added. "The sun's already been up for two whole minutes."

Blossom sighed. "Only little kids get up early on the weekend," she said.

"But you always get up with us," Bubbles said, pouting.

"Well, not anymore," Blossom said haughtily. "I've grown out of that." She lay down and pulled the blanket over her head.

"You mean you don't want to play with us now?" Bubbles sounded hurt.

"Come on, Bubbles," Buttercup muttered. "Let's go downstairs. We'll let Sleeping Boring have the whole bed to herself."

Blossom listened as her sisters left the room. She stretched out her arms and her legs. It felt great not to have to share the bed with anyone.

An hour later, Blossom found the Professor and her sisters finishing breakfast in the kitchen.

"Well, good morning, sleepy-head!" the Professor sang out cheerfully.

Blossom rolled her eyes. "Please, Professor," she said. "I'm too old for babyish nicknames, you know that."

The Professor looked disappointed. "But you always liked when I . . ." He stopped. "All right, Blossom, if you feel you're too old for nicknames, I understand. Now, how about breakfast? Would you like some nice sweet pancakes?"

Blossom yawned. "Oh, no thanks. I'll just take coffee."

Bubbles and Buttercup stared at her. "Coffee?!" they yelled.

"You don't drink coffee, Blossom," Bubbles said.

Blossom shrugged. "I do now."

The Professor looked concerned. "Well, all right, Blossom, if you want to try a little bit of coffee, I'll let you. But I don't think you'll like it." He poured a tiny bit of coffee into a cup.

Blossom tasted the coffee. It was terrible! But she wasn't about to admit that. "Mmmm! Delicious!"

"Professor," she continued in her most businesslike voice, "there's something I need to discuss with you."

18

"Certainly, Blossom," the Professor replied. "What is it?"

"I've decided that I'm ready to have my own bed," Blossom said.

"But Blossom!" Bubbles cried. Her mouth was trembling. "You always sleep with us!"

"Well, I don't want to anymore," Blossom said. "I'm too old for that now."

"But we're the same age as you," Buttercup objected. "What makes you think you're so grown-up all of a sudden?"

"Some people mature faster than others," Blossom said, tossing her red hair. "I just happen to be very grown-up for my age."

The Professor's forehead creased. "Well, I suppose if you feel you'd rather sleep on your own . . ."

"Good," Blossom said. "I knew you'd see it my way."

"But Blossom," the Professor said, still sounding worried, "I don't know if we can fit another bed into you Girls' room."

"I don't want to sleep in there anyway. Let's put it in the laboratory."

"My laboratory?" The Professor's eyes widened in surprise. "But I work in there."

"You won't be working at night when I'm sleeping, Professor," Blossom pointed out. "Besides, I'm getting to the age where I need a room of my own."

"Well, I suppose we could try it. . . ." the Professor said.

What? The Powerpuff Girls sleeping in separate bedrooms? But that's unnatural! What next? Fish without schools? Wolves without packs? Peanut butter without jelly?

chapter 3

Later that night . . .

Bubbles and Buttercup lay in bed. The Professor had already kissed them good night, and they were all tucked in.

But something felt strange. Neither one of them could get to sleep.

After a while, Bubbles began to whimper. "I miss Blossom," she said.

Buttercup rolled over. "Well, get over it," she said. "Blossom says she's so grown-up. She thinks she doesn't need us anymore. So we shouldn't need her."

"I guess you're right," Bubbles sniffed. "But I still miss her."

"The bed does feel kind of big," Buttercup admitted. She sat up. "Come on, let's make a fort out of the pillows and pretend we're being attacked by a vicious enemy army that wants to tear us limb from limb. That ought to cheer you up."

Bubbles brightened. "Okay."

Meanwhile, downstairs in the laboratory . . .

Blossom changed into her pink nightgown and climbed into her new single bed. She sat propped up against her pillows and looked around happily. She felt so independent and grown-up.

The Professor poked his head in.

"Good night, sweet — I mean, good night, Blossom," he said. "Do you want me to read you a story before you go to sleep?"

Blossom thought a moment. "How about something from the newspaper?" she suggested.

The Professor looked surprised. "The newspaper? Really? I didn't know you were so interested in the news, Blossom."

Blossom nodded. "Oh, yes. I think the news is so much more mature than story-books."

"Well, if you're sure," the Professor said. He got his copy of the *Townsville Times*. He began reading Blossom an article about Townsville's plans to install new stop signs at intersections.

Before she knew it, Blossom could feel

her eyelids drooping. Soon she was sound asleep.

The next morning . . .

Blossom sat at the kitchen table with her coffee cup. Bubbles and Buttercup were devouring mounds of blueberry pancakes with whipped cream.

"Mmmm," Buttercup said. She wiped

her face with the back of her arm. "These are delicious, Professor."

"Are you sure you don't want some, Blossom?" Bubbles asked. "I'll share mine with you."

"No, thanks," Blossom replied, stirring her coffee. "I grew out of pancakes and stuff like that."

Buttercup drank the last of her milk. "Hey, Girls, want to go outside and play ball?" she asked impatiently.

"Ball is for babies," Blossom said with her chin in the air.

Buttercup rolled her eyes. "Whatever."

"I'll play with you, Buttercup," Bubbles said. "Come on, let's go!"

The two Girls ran out the door together.

Blossom looked around the kitchen.
What did grown-ups do all day, anyway? "So,
Professor," she said, "what's new? Tell me
about the experiments you've been doing
lately."

"Well, I've been investigating the rela-
tionship between alpha polarization and
proton energetics," the Professor explained eagerly. "I'm particularly interested in the way they might interact with
the equations of kinematics and . . ."

Blossom played with the edge of her
dress as the Professor's voice went on and
on. She looked around the room.

". . . X rays of supernovas in optimum
stratospheric conditions," the Professor
continued excitedly. "And, of course, that

brings into question the whole notion of the heredity hypothesis and what role it plays in the spectral observations of . . ."

Poor Blossom. Once the Professor gets going, it's pretty hard to stop him.

A little while later, Bubbles and Buttercup came skipping in from outside.

". . . properties of sodium aluminate and the — oh, hello, Girls," the Professor said. "Did you have fun playing ball?"

Buttercup nodded. "We sure did."

"Now we want to color," Bubbles said.

"Want to help us, Blossom?" Buttercup asked.

"No, thanks!" Blossom scoffed. "I'm too old for that sort of thing."

"Are you sure?" Buttercup taunted. "Afterward we're going to have ice-cream cones."

"With cherries on top!" Bubbles added excitedly. "Come on, Blossom! You can have strawberry, your favorite."

Blossom yawned. "No, thanks. I'm not interested."

Buttercup looked angry. "I guess you're only interested in grown-up stuff now, huh?"

"Actually, Blossom and I were having a very nice grown-up conversation," the Professor explained. "Blossom, we can get back to our talk in a minute, right after I help your sisters set up their crayons."

"Uh, that's okay, Professor," Blossom said. "I think I have something important I have to take care of right now." She hurried out of the room.

Blossom hesitated a moment, and then headed for the Professor's laboratory. She flopped down on her bed and looked around her new room. Being a grown-up could be really boring if all you did was talk. If only there was something mature she could spend time on . . .

Suddenly, Blossom had an idea. She ran to the hallway and grabbed a thick yellow book. She began turning the pages quickly.

What are you doing with that Townsville telephone book, Blossom? What are you up to now?

30

chapter 4

The next day at the Utonium household . . .
It's another pleasant morning. The sun is
shining, and all is peaceful and —
Bang! Bang! Bang!
Hey, what's all that racket?
Bang! Bang! Whirrr! Whirrr! Screech!
Who's making all that noise? And what are
all those trucks and vans doing parked outside
the house? And what are all those workers do-
ing marching in and out the front door with
tools hanging from their belts?

Blossom stood in the middle of the living room with a clipboard. She was yelling directions at the workers.

A workman with a huge spool of wire walked up to her.

"You in charge here, miss?" he asked.

"Yes, I am," Blossom answered.

"I'm here to put in the new phone line," the man explained. "Where do you want it?"

"Come with me," Blossom replied.

She led the man down to the Professor's laboratory. Painters stood on ladders, brushing a fresh coat of pink onto the walls and ceiling. A carpet-layer was rolling out new, rose-colored wall-to-wall carpeting.

"You can put the new phone right here," Blossom said, pointing to the shiny new red desk.

"Okay, sure thing," the man answered, getting to work.

Just then, the Professor came running in with Bubbles and Buttercup close behind him.

"Blossom!" the Professor cried, throwing his hands up into the air. "What's going on in here? What are you doing?"

"Just making a few changes, Professor," Blossom said. She called up to one of the painters. "Hey, watch what you're doing! That pink is only for the walls. The trim is supposed to be cherry red, remember?" She sighed and looked around. "I can't believe the window-treatment people still aren't here! They were supposed to install my diagonal blinds hours ago!"

Bubbles looked stunned. "You're getting diagonal blinds?"

Blossom nodded. "Scarlet red. They're going to look great."

"But Blossom! This is my laboratory!" the Professor objected. "I have to work in here!"

"Well, I'm sorry, Professor, but it also

happens to be my room!" Blossom pointed out. "Besides, I'm going to be working in here from now on, too. I'm having my own phone installed — my own hotline."

"But we already have a hotline," Buttercup objected.

"That's right, Blossom. You've always shared a hotline with your sisters," the Professor added.

"Those days are over," Blossom said firmly. She turned to her sisters. "Sorry, Girls, but you spend too much time playing and doing silly kid stuff to be serious crime fighters. You were just dragging me down. I'm in business for myself now."

Two workmen walked in carrying a huge sign. The sign read: BLOSSOM'S BIG-TIME CRIME-BUSTING BUREAU.

"You can put that right over the door," Blossom directed the workers. She turned to the Professor and the Girls and smiled. "As of today, the citizens of Townsville have a choice!"

Bubbles's big blue eyes grew watery. "B-but Blossom . . ."

"You can't do that!" Buttercup yelled.

"Well, it looks like I just did, doesn't it?" Blossom said with a shrug.

Buttercup yanked angrily on the Professor's lab coat. "Professor, we have to talk to you right away."

The Professor stood motionless, staring at his former laboratory. His mouth hung open.

"Right away!" Buttercup repeated. She pulled the Professor by his lab coat. "Come on, Bubbles!" she called.

A moment later, Buttercup, Bubbles, and the Professor huddled together in the living room.

"We have to stop her," Buttercup said angrily. "We can't let Blossom do this."

"We certainly can't," the Professor agreed. "I need my laboratory back."

"And we need our sister back," Bubbles added.

"Just go tell her she can't do it, Professor!" Buttercup demanded. "Go make her take all that stuff down and start acting normal!"

The Professor shook his head. "Girls, I may be able to force Blossom to repaint the lab and take out her phone —"

"Okay," Bubbles said.

"Go for it, Professor," Buttercup agreed.

"But that won't make her start behaving like your sister again." The Professor smiled. "I think I have a better plan."

He bent forward and started whispering to them.

Whatever this plan is, it had better be a good one, Professor! Blossom is definitely getting out of control.

Chapter 5

"We're going to Kiddy Land! We're going to Kiddy Land!" Bubbles sang out happily.

Buttercup sat on the couch, studying a brochure. "Oh, wow! Look at this! It's the biggest roller coaster in the world! It's called the Monster Coaster. Let's go on the Monster Coaster first!"

"No, let's get cotton candy first," Bubbles suggested. "Let's get tons of pretty pink cotton candy and eat it all up!"

"And *then* let's go on the Monster Coaster!" Buttercup cried.

"Monster Coaster! Monster Coaster! Yay!" the two Girls yelled together.

The Professor came into the room. He held Bubbles's blue suitcase in one hand and Buttercup's green one in the other.

"You Girls remembered to pack your

bathing suits in here, didn't you?" the Professor asked. "You don't want to miss out on the seven-hundred-foot pool with the twenty water slides, do you?"

"We remembered," Bubbles and Buttercup sang out together.

Blossom sat on a chair with her arms folded across her chest.

"Blossom, are you sure you don't want to come to Kiddy Land with your sisters?" the Professor asked.

"No, thanks," Blossom said. "Kiddy Land is for little kids." She tossed her head. "I'll be just fine here on my own."

"Well, just to be sure, I've asked the Mayor to come stay for a while," the Professor said. "Although I'm sure you can handle everything by yourself, Blossom."

The doorbell rang.

"That must be the Mayor now," the Professor said. He opened the front door.

"Hello, everyone!" the Mayor said.

"Hello, Mayor," the Professor replied. "Thanks for coming. Well, Girls, we'd better get going now. Mayor, Blossom knows where everything is. Just ask her if you need anything."

"That's right," Blossom said, her chest puffing out with pride. "I can do practically everything on my own."

"Oh, I'm sure you can," the Mayor said. He chuckled. "Why, I'll bet you'll be the one taking care of me, Blossom."

Blossom smiled. "You can count on me, Mayor!"

Later that evening!

"That was a delicious dinner, Blossom!" the Mayor said. "Those were the best peanut butter and jelly sandwiches I've ever had."

Blossom beamed. "Why, thank you, Mayor. They're my specialty."

"I'm stuffed." The Mayor patted his belly. "I think I'll go relax in the other room while you clean up."

Poor Blossom. Isn't the Mayor going to help you with the dishes? Well, you did tell him you could handle everything on your own. . . .

Even with her super cleaning powers, it was very late by the time Blossom finished cleaning in the kitchen. She found the Mayor asleep on a chair in the living room. She got a blanket and spread it out over the snoring politician. Then she went to her room to tuck herself into bed.

The next day!

Blossom got out of bed and started to get dressed. As she looked through her dresser, she realized that she was out of clean white tights.

She flew into the living room with no shoes or stockings. The Mayor was still asleep in the chair.

"Mayor!" Blossom shook his shoulder. "Mayor, wake up!"

The Mayor opened his eyes with a start.

He jumped out of the chair. "Aaah! What? What is it? What happened?"

"Mayor, I don't have any clean tights," Blossom explained.

"Whew! You scared me," the Mayor said. He sat back down with a sigh. "Well, I guess you'll have to do the laundry, Blossom. Oh, and after you're done, I'll have my breakfast, please."

Poor Blossom! Being responsible for everything isn't so much fun, is it?

Just then something dropped through the mail slot in the door and landed on the floor. Blossom flew over and picked it up. It was a postcard. On one side of the postcard was a picture of a giant trampoline with kids jumping on it. On the back it said: *Having a great time! Miss you! Love, Bubbles, Buttercup, and the Professor.*

The next day!

Blossom flew into the living room. The Mayor was sitting on the couch, watching cartoons. He was crunching on candy. On the floor was a mountain of candy wrappers.

"Mayor!" Blossom cried. "You're making a mess!"

"Sssh!" the Mayor hissed. "This is a really good part." He went back to watching TV.

With a sigh, Blossom cleaned up the candy wrappers from the floor.

"Mayor, you're going to ruin your appetite," she said. "I'm making dinner soon."

The phone rang. The Mayor leaned over and picked it up. "I hate it when that happens," he muttered.

"Yes? Oh, hi, Ms. Bellum," the Mayor said, bored. "Yes, I see. Okay, I'll take care of it." He turned to Blossom. "There's a monster attacking Townsville." He smiled. "This is so convenient, Blossom. I don't even have to use the hotline to get in touch with you. Well, good luck with the monster. Oh, and can you pick up some more of those peanut clusters on your way home? They're delicious!" He went back to watching TV.

Well, Blossom, it looks like you're on your own again!

Chapter 6

Blossom flew toward the center of Townsville. There were wrecked buildings and broken streetlights everywhere.

A scaly monster with a dragonlike head stood in the middle of Townsville Central Park. People ran screaming as the monster tossed picnic tables over his shoulder and laughed.

Blossom took a deep breath. It was up to her to save Townsville. She had to prove she could defend the city on her own.

Summoning all her strength, Blossom flew toward the monster. She landed hard on his scaly neck.

The monster bucked, trying to shake her off. Blossom hung on with everything she had, but she wasn't strong enough to control the monster by herself. If only Buttercup were there to wallop him!

The monster gave a violent shake, and she tumbled to the ground. Then he ran off through the park, wildly stomping trees and bushes.

Blossom looked around. Nearby, a group of kids were riding on a carousel. Seeing the kids having fun reminded Blossom of her sisters away at Kiddy Land. She sighed.

Suddenly, the monster changed direction and headed straight for the carousel. The kids began to scream.

Blossom flew into action! She ripped a tree out by its roots and laid it in the monster's path. He tripped and went flying. But moments later the monster was up again.

Blossom sighed. Fighting the monster by herself was exhausting. If only her sisters were here to help her! Sure, they were a nuisance sometimes, but they were tough and strong.

The monster grabbed the carousel and

ripped it out of the ground. He set it on his scaly finger and began to twirl it at top speed. Screaming children were thrown off in every direction.

Oh, no, Blossom! Quick, save the kids!

Gathering all her superspeed, Blossom flew off to catch the children. She managed to get them all to safety.

Then she turned to face the monster. "You are ruining everyone's day at the park!" she yelled. "Stop it right now!"

Blossom shot bright pink eye beams at the monster. He fell backward and collapsed on the ground.

The crowd began to cheer. But Blossom hardly noticed. She was too tired.

With her eyes half-closed, Blossom flew back home. She found the Mayor in the kitchen, surrounded by a huge mess.

Food and dirty dishes were all over every counter.

"Mayor!" Blossom cried. "What happened? What did you do?"

"Blossom! I got hungry, and you weren't home in time to fix my dinner!" the Mayor complained. "But at least you're here to take care of things now."

Blossom sighed.

Poor Blossom. Tired of being a grown-up?

The phone rang. Blossom answered it. "Hello?"

"Hi, Blossom," said the Professor.

"Professor!" Blossom was so happy to hear his voice.

"How are you doing?" the Professor asked.

"Okay, I guess," Blossom answered.

"You don't sound so good," the Professor asked. "Is everything all right?"

"Everything's fine, Professor," Blossom answered. She was too tired and sad to tell the Professor everything that had happened. "Are you coming home soon?"

"Not for a few more days," the Professor said. "Everyone's having such a good time here. Your sisters say hi!"

"Okay, well, tell them I say hi, too," Blossom said. "Bye, Professor." She hung up the phone. She felt so lonely. She missed her family so much. She didn't want to be a grown-up anymore.

chapter 7

The next day!

Blossom sat on her bed.

Wait a minute, Blossom, that's not your bed! Not anymore! That's your sisters' bed! What about your fancy new room?

On the nightstand was the postcard from her family. Blossom looked at it again wistfully. She felt lonely. Suddenly, the idea of trying to be a grown-up seemed really dumb.

"Blossom!" the Mayor called from downstairs. "Blossom!"

Blossom sighed. The Mayor probably wanted her to fix him a snack. She put down the postcard and floated downstairs. "What is it, Mayor?"

To her surprise, the Professor, Bubbles, and Buttercup were standing there. "You came home!" Blossom said, surprised. "You ended your vacation early!"

"Nope. We came back because we need your help," Bubbles said.

"That's right," Buttercup added. "There's a huge monster in Kiddy Land!"

"Really? Okay! I'm ready to go!" Blossom cried happily. "Just lead the way."

Go, Blossom, go! Even fighting a monster with your sisters will feel like a vacation after the way things have been going on your own!

55

But when The Powerpuff Girls and the Professor arrived in Kiddy Land, there was no monster in sight. Blossom was confused. All around her, families were strolling, eating goodies, and lining up for rides.

"Where's the monster?" Blossom asked.

"Right over there," Bubbles giggled.

Buttercup grabbed Blossom's arm and began to pull her. "Come on!"

In front of Blossom was a sign that read: MONSTER COASTER. THE BIGGEST ROLLER COASTER IN THE WORLD. RIDE IT IF YOU DARE!

"The Girls didn't want to try to tackle this 'monster' without you, Blossom," the Professor said with a chuckle.

Blossom turned to her sisters. "I'm sorry about the way I acted," she said. "I thought I was being grown-up. But I was really just being selfish."

"That's okay," Bubbles said. "We're just glad to have you back."

"Yeah," Buttercup agreed.

"I'm glad to be back!" Blossom said. "Living with the Mayor was the worst."

"Well, Girls, are you ready to go on the ride?" the Professor asked.

"Monster Coaster! Monster Coaster! Yay!" Blossom, Bubbles, and Buttercup yelled together, jumping up and down.

Aww, look at Blossom, Bubbles, and Buttercup. We know they'll have fun tackling all kinds of monsters — TOGETHER.

So once again, the day is saved, thanks to The Powerpuff Girls!